Utopia

J. Rod

Aurora Gabriela surprised me with her question, one rainy day in September:

- Would you be afraid that the end of the world was coming? - He told me looking into my eyes, with his pupils shining with concern.

- I did not answer-. The world ends for many people every day when they take their last breath and their heart stops beating.

She nodded her head and leaned against me feeling safe. I took another sip from my cup of coffee, watching and listening to the raindrops hit the window, blurring the trees.

Years later, without her, I realized that the world ended for me the moment she was no longer close to me. Everyone has their world, their little piece of the world.

Chapter 1

Have you ever noticed the effects caused by the moon in every part of your body? Or how does it influence the behavior of other people?

Those rare days, when you wake up depressed, listless, without an explanation to justify it. You could almost ensure that it is an external effect in the environment, like something floating in the atmosphere causing inexplicable sensations in you.

That same effect sometimes gives you a deep peace that when looking at the sky at night radiates a relaxing energy in every muscle. You can feel it in every breath of the fresh air around you.

Sometimes it also causes overflowing joy, as if a ray of happiness penetrated the depths of our being.

Sometimes that outward feeling brings tears to your eyes at the slightest thought, leaving you vulnerable to any external stimuli. You can't explain it, you can't find the words, you just perceive it and you get used to living with those sensations, just as you've gotten used to breathing and feeling your heart beat from the moment you were conceived.

Countless scientific studies have observed these changes, without finding any explanation for it, however, we know that everything influences our mood, and other living beings also have an influence on us, our minds and behavior.

Water, the sun, the moon, the magnetism of the Earth, the consciousness of people and many other factors have been studied for centuries to understand the power of their energy and influence on human beings.

At a certain age, I still thought it was quackery, but it was shocking to discover scientific experiments on those events. I could no longer evade the discussion with my argument of being a man of science, despite the fact that this discipline has discovered things unimaginable by our minds.

Perhaps we are just one more cog in a higher machinery, like a microscopic organism forming one of greater complexity together with the Earth and the universe, a being that lives with other beings of unimaginable and invisible size because its immense dimension exceeds our capacity and range. Of vision.

Hundreds of thousands of people die in the world. Some because of a natural disaster, such as an earthquake or tidal wave. And each body is degraded until it becomes dust that will fertilize the earth like any other process in nature.

Sometimes I would like to think that human beings are the neurons of that Superior being, where thought originates. We have always boasted of being the only rational animal on Earth, and this reasoning capacity may be due to the fact that our function is to synapse with the billions of people who inhabit the planet, thus developing new creations and complex thoughts.

Probably, when we die we are one less cell in the central nervous system that stops working, just as millions of neurons perish daily in our brain, due to alcohol, drugs, stress, chemicals or blows. And just as we have hundreds of millions of them in our brain, the Higher Self could have billions of us connecting every moment to come up with a simple reasoning, say yes or no to the creation of another universe given the circumstances of resources. and capacity. Or say, yes or no, to use or obtain energy by feeding on other sources such as the sun, the wind or magnetism.

Or perhaps we are something harmful in that Supreme Being, a virus within that organism replicating millions of times until it destroys everything in its path as we have done with every part of the Earth.

Perhaps the wind is the breath of that Superior Being, which, like us, fills our body with life and nourishes each cell with energy to carry out even the slightest thought and our planet is one more organ of that infinite body: the energy feeding every remote corner of the earth.

For this reason, the new theories, about how we influence our body and mind as if it were a magnetic field on other people, perhaps have gained such popularity because those concepts that we did not understand before behaved like a group of beings that interact with each other through millions, as do the neurons in our brain.

And just as that energy is linked to improve or worsen the world and make good or bad decisions, so, this supreme being -which is not God, because he is still of unimaginable and unquantifiable size-, synapses with us to move the world.

In other times, we visualized how esotericism or spirituality was transformed into science, into research about each of the things that seemed inexplicable in our lives, such as the vibration of human beings, also called quantum physics.

Among so many confusing theories, the most insane one I have ever heard appeared to become part of my life.

His theory was so simple, yet implausible, that it bordered on madness.

Episode 2

When I was born, I was one of four billion people who inhabited the world in 1976. Today, 45 years later, I am one of eight billion people. Which makes me think that I am less significant today, half as important to the planet as I was four decades ago.

I was studying the last semester of my medical degree at the Universidad de Sotavento. The world seemed overnight to start convulsing. The increase in hurricanes, earthquakes, tsunamis, sinkholes, floods, extreme frosts, suffocating heat or inexplicable wars was normal. The world was already beginning to include the environment as a main issue on the agenda. However, we humans seemed engaged in destroying the Earth and therefore ourselves, as illogical and stupid as it reads.

Some pointed to the apocalyptic prophecies of the Bible and some to older ones. Others attributed the deterioration to a greater social unconsciousness about respect for the environment that had exponentially damaged the world by each person over the years. Only she in her head, flooded with complex ideas, spoke out for her famous "inevitability".

Yes, I know, it sounds strange, but that's how I discovered it one spring day, with the sun falling gently on the waves of the Atlantic. I was standing outside the school watching the horizon and pouring the last drops of coffee from my metal thermos into my mouth. That wasn't the most bitter thing I tasted that day, but her words debating with me, as if I cared what she thought at that moment when she was just another student in my class. And the way in which he interfered in the conversation I was having with Aurora, my platonic love since the beginning of my degree, and some of her friends was even more bitter. A rude intrusion I still remember.

- Adrián Manu, you can't avoid it, the decision has been made – she said as she left behind Claudia, standing between us, who were chatting about the implications of global warming. Unless we evolve and can breathe underwater, we can be part of the new world.

His words at first made me angry. Although the fact that he mentioned my full name made me happy, however, his intrusion was daring, but analyzing them a bit, I thought of laughing, but then they generated an indescribable doubt about the concepts we know today.

The other girls were just incredulous and called her crazy, but her way of expressing it seemed so real to me that it caused me a bit of stress to think that it was true.

- Whose decision? - I told him with a sarcasm gesture. Annoyed, Adela turned to see me, insinuating with her eyes that I should ignore her so that she could continue on her way.

- Well, of the being where human beings inhabit.

Just that comment was enough for the girls to walk away, without saying goodbye, with a mocking gesture and leave the two of us alone debating, in the middle of the intense rays of the sun. At first I stayed listening to it. It didn't seem polite to me to leave her talking to herself and also because I was still waiting for my older sister to pick me up to go home.

- You mean God? - I told him trying to guess his statements.

- No, we do not form God, he is infinite. - he replied, further confusing my thoughts on the subject.

- So, I definitely don't understand who you mean.

I took my backpack and walked towards the bathroom to try to get rid of it, but he raised his voice getting closer to me, forcing me to stay so as not to be rude.

- We are only part of a superior being- Aurora told me while I looked at her and tried to understand her words-, as well as the microorganisms that live inside our bodies.

- And, then, what is your theory to counteract climate change? - I told her a little annoyed, challenging her to give me an acceptable solution. She frowned in annoyance.

- There is no way to achieve that, although it sounds totalitarian or dramatic, but it is the truth. It is impossible to counteract climate change.

She said it with such certainty that it made me think a little about the credibility of her statements, otherwise I would doubt her mental health, and in my experience with her she had never shown signs like that, on the contrary, she was always a very modest girl and applied to studies.

- So, your point of view goes against the universal truth, to take care of the planet, to have the necessary conditions for human life.

- It is a universal truth within the context that we currently know because we believe that the universe revolves around us - she said ironically, while cleaning her glasses clouded by the heat.

- So what you think is above the laws discovered by the most brilliant scientists? - I refuted him as his absurd way of wanting to be right at all costs began to despair me.

- Okay, so what Claudia says is a new law that discards the previous ones by magic: trees do not purify the air, climate change does not exist, ... - I said.

- Obviously not; It is only a theory that I have arrived at after reading several authors; you have to analyze the information and anyone could reach that conclusion. Most of the things we believed in the past have been disproved.

- Imagine, if everyone believed in your theory, no person or industry would do the least to reduce their polluting emissions- I told him appealing to a forceful argument.

"Believe me, I know, but they are mutually exclusive events." Now he appealed to his knowledge of probability and statistics to make me look ignorant. I am also an environmentalist. I began to do so out of empathy with all the beings on the planet, but it is something inevitable, whether we stop producing plastics in the world, reduce environmental pollution, recycle, completely reforest the planet or pray, nothing will prevent the old body from and sick, in which we live, perish.

I knew that she was an environmentalist, she always recycled the smallest object, plus I had seen her actively participate in multiple causes to care for the environment.

"Then, I will be able to sleep peacefully, knowing that I no longer have to separate the organic and inorganic garbage" I told her smiling and trying to be nice to her to say goodbye sarcastically.

Aurora answered me promptly:

-It's like when you want to lose weight to improve your state of health and you start any of the diets that are promoted: Keto, Tb12, The Zone, Intermittent Fasting, Ultrametabolism or Accelerate your Metabolism. But there comes a time when your body is so deteriorated that no diet or treatment will work. The being to which we belong is sick and can no longer eliminate excess fluid in its body, which is why the flood of the entire Earth is imminent.

Soon after her father parked his car right next to us and she drove off. I thought she would be upset by that last joke of mine and it was I who was overwhelmed by that last nonsense, but which, nevertheless, largely coincided with the increasingly recurring natural disasters.

Chapter 3

Several weeks passed and she continued her attempt to change our minds, but instead she only got more taunts and indifference from the other girls. At times I stayed to analyze her strange arguments for a bit and to live with her a little more, which I hadn't done in all the years as classmates. Something had started to catch my attention a bit about that "nerdy" girl obsessed with that crazy apocalyptic theory. Aurora dressed in a strange way, without an ounce of makeup, which allowed us to appreciate her natural beauty. The other girls were unrecognizable, without retouching or using filters on all their social media photos, but she was simple. You didn't find her attractive. You had to stare at each of its details. His short hair obscured his lack of styling, and his body was slim, short, though little noticeable because of his conservative dress. She had a perfect formation of her gifted chest; her wide hips managed to stand out despite the baggy pants she liked so much, and her thick legs managed to stand out in the hideous blue jean skirt of the uniform. His nose wasn't flat or long, but it wasn't upturned either, just nice and normal size. His eyes weren't big or colored anyway, but his gaze was always sincere, as was his way of speaking, perhaps at certain times even irritating due to his sincerity, like on that occasion when we discussed the subject again.

- Don't be ignorant- his description of my person touched me deeply. All scientific theories point to not even having fifty percent reproducibility. How do you explain that?

And, really, she was right in that I couldn't explain that piece of information she provided and that if it was true it would put me in check.

He did not know his sources, and at times he thought he was inventing or fantasizing.

- And where can I get scientific evidence of what you say? - I expressed to him.

For the first time I tried to take an interest in something she was telling me so that I could discuss it further and get to know her more. I figured my question would embarrass her a bit.

- Of course I am not referring to the magazines that your friends read, like Hola or Vogue, nor to the library of our university or the country you will find something. Or perhaps we distinguish ourselves by being a country that promotes science? You should search in digital libraries of first world universities.

He had already called me ignorant for not knowing where to look for information, now also for not knowing where to look for it.

- And how are you so sure of what you affirm? - I told her as if she were a defendant and had to prove the veracity of her statement.

- A study in the journal Nature showed that 70 percent of scientists are unsuccessful in reproducing experiments conducted by other researchers in different years and latitudes.

I had no other argument left but to try to minimize theirs:

- I would have to read that study to know if what you are telling me is true.

My comment made Aurora very angry. I noticed it because his brow furrowed and with his gaze he seemed to be trying to make me disappear.

- You don't believe me then? – She asked me annoyed as if she was questioning her honor, not just that of a scientific publication.

- I would like to believe you, but I don't have enough evidence for it.

That was like a kick to his pride. And immediately, very upset, she began to search desperately with her pupils on inside her backpack with images of stars and planets. He found that magazine with the crumpled pages as a sign of having been read many times, Nature magazine number 127. He opened it to page 14, where he began the synopsis of the study carried out.

- Here you are, ignoramus!

Her insult more than annoyed me, made me laugh and made her blush even more. He threw the magazine at me and hit me in the chest.

I took it in my hands and read it carefully. There it was explained in a detailed and rigorous way how this study had been carried out.

- Okay, you win, but even so your theory still seems crazy to me- I really don't know what motivated me to express the following words; I think it was more an attempt to redress my doubts towards her than to have a more sustainable explanation. I have an idea, why don't we get together on Friday for ice cream and you keep telling me more about that theory so I can understand it?

She looked at me surprised by my invitation and clarified:

- But it will only be a professional matter, we will not go out as if it were a date.

- As you say, what time are you free?

- At six in the evening I leave my piano class. You can come in at that time.

- Perfect!

Chapter 4

I had to think about what an ideal scientific appointment would be like; a couple of days ago they had inaugurated the city museum right in front of the sea. For her, it would be very attractive, and for me to have her slant-eyed look facing the sea, too.

It was the part where the river forks with the sea, and that gave the place a more original tint. I went to look for her five minutes before the agreed time to avoid my nerves by breathing some fresh air from the breeze.

At what point had the nerdy girl in the room become my date? That was one of the questions that overwhelmed me and caused even more sweating on my hands and on my forehead catalyzed by the immense heat.

I had always seen her with that horrible school skirt, with a blouse with a large shield; socks up to the knees, old glasses with great magnification and a ponytail collecting her hair.

Leaving the piano class I could barely recognize her. He didn't wear his usual glasses, and I discovered that he had dark blue eyes like the sea at sunset. Instead of the traditional hideous school skirt, she wore a tight black one that exposed her perfect hips. A white blouse with ruffles and something that captivated instantly was her loose hair, with black sneakers, it was the typical dress for a piano recital.

Aurora approached me and I could barely hide how tense I was to admire her and go out with her. Stuttering I was able to address her.

- Good afternoon, Aurora. How are you?

She looked at me with a surprised face, as if she had forgotten our date or meeting.

- Hello, good afternoon, I had forgotten our meeting to continue teaching you about science.

Sometimes his sarcasm wasn't as pretty as his look, without those horrible glasses. But I had to endure his attacks.

- If you have time? - I asked with a broken voice, waiting for a possible refusal.

- Little, but I think that in an hour we can return, because I will accompany my parents to a dinner with my uncles for their birthday.

My excitement at thinking that seeing her so pretty that day was because of me, vanished when I found out that she had an important family gathering. I went into a nervous state of not knowing what to do or say before her beautiful but lacerating gaze.

"Okay, okay," I stammered again. Can we go in my car or do we walk? The museum was five blocks from the building where he took piano lessons; walking would make me look less nervous than getting into my car where I've never gotten into a girl before.

- Let's go in your car, it's still very hot.

His answer chilled me; On the way to the car, she didn't know whether to open the door for her, or perhaps she was one of the modern women who is annoyed by these attitudes. He didn't know what to do and he didn't want to make her uncomfortable.

So even though it seemed stupid, I decided to ask:

- Do you like to open the door or do it yourself?

- My question surprised him, he frowned and delicately answered me:

- Opening the door is the task of every gentleman, but considering that ours is not a date, but a scientific meeting, he left it to your free will.

If I opened her door for her, it was the most subtle way of showing her that I liked seeing her, so with my hands sweating from nerves and the intense heat, I walked in front of her and pulled the handle of the passenger door, indicating with my left that she should enter. .

- Thank you very much, Manu- he told me, winking at me in such a way that that image remained permanently impregnated in my mind.

We spent an hour going through each of the levels of the museum and she explained to me so many things that I didn't know about the history of our city; He just wanted to get to the top floor to drink an espresso with a view of the sea and his pupils.

We finally got to the cafeteria and I immediately chose the terrace to feel the natural breeze and the aroma of the coffee. She ordered a double espresso, and I thought she would go for a sweet and cold drink, but, no, she loved the intense flavor of this caffeine elixir.

- So, do you believe in my theory? - he questioned me releasing a masterful smile that he could not rebuff.

- Yes, I believe her- I told him, although I wasn't completely convinced-, but it scares me to think about her, what would be the way to follow then? Do nothing?

Aurora stared at me, with the rays of light shining even brighter her turquoise blue pupils. His answer made me in a few words rethink my whole life, stop worrying about the future and live in the present.

- Be happy and that's it.

Chapter 5

Looking for more information about the Theory of Energy I started reading about quantum physics topics. It was an exciting world, with complex things, for me and many students. It seemed similar to what he had said, since some of his ideas were that humans can change matter and that we are not independent or autonomous, but rather belong to a system. If we are all connected by energy in the same system, we are probably part of a greater being, and perhaps its neurons synapse to create.

In a book by one of the best-selling authors on Amazon, Dawson Church, I was introduced to a concept called Collective Global Consciousness. From what little I was able to understand is that an event is influenced by those who observe it. As well as if we have something positive in mind, we generate good things and vice versa.

These ideas, although I still could not understand them, began to give me a guideline to generate a proposal to counteract climate change following the patterns of Dawson's theory.

- And, then, what should we do?, sit back and finish what's left of the planet?, drink beer until the world ends? - I asked him while we were sitting on the terrace of the school cafeteria.

"It wouldn't be a bad option, although I prefer Chilean Carmenere wine, while you drink beer," he told me while giving me a wink and leaving me thinking about the possibility of flirting, although the most emotional thing was that for the first time he was beginning to be nice to me.

I thought it was time to show you my acquired knowledge on the subject.

I quoted from memory a theory by Max Planck, father of quantum physics: "all matter originates and exists only by virtue of a force that makes the particles of an atom vibrate and holds together the tiny solar system that composes it. We must assume that behind that force there is a conscious and intelligent mind. This Mind is the matrix of all matter.

- I see that you are advancing in the vast world of this science- he replied and I was excited when I noticed for the first time a possible intention to be nice to me. I didn't want to fantasize.

We talked for hours, not only about his theory, he also told me about his family, about his parents, who became boyfriends in elementary school, and were still together. Of his two younger sisters, whom he adored, and with whom he played board games all night. We spent a wonderful afternoon, more and more agreed with his unthinkable ideas.

On the one hand, they seemed very strange to me, but on the other hand, I had no scientific way to refute them, nor did I want to. I just wanted to talk to her for hours. It all seemed true despite not believing it possible. And more when it came out of those beautiful thick lips and were founded with his penetrating gaze.

- I wish we were like a virus replicating in order to maintain the species, but we are doomed to extinction and not only due to the external effects of the climate. We are a type of virus that goes against logic and rationality, that goes extinct with wars, abortions, poverty. What animal or living being would take an embryo of its own from life? Neither.

Her words were forceful, she was pro-life, which also automatically made me so. Without realizing it I was becoming a follower of his ideas, like a religious parishioner, but in this case of his religion of ideas.

That day I chose to establish a watershed in our relationship as teammates and see if it could transcend.

- Can we go to the city symphony concert tonight? - I released without further ado waiting for a resounding no or a yes of an official appointment. She thought for a few seconds before answering.

- Yes, pick me up an hour before.

An indescribable emotion ran through my body. We already had a formal date, and every time I knew more about her my affection towards her increased.

And that small achievement triggered more frequent appointments on the terrace of the museum and with a longer duration. Sometimes we lost track of time.

What started with several heated discussions between her and me turned into hours of infinite happiness, laughing with her over any detail. Until that day when everything changed.

Chapter 6

Our meetings were more frequent and I was looking to intensify them before the winter break arrived at the university and I had less contact with her.

That February fifteenth will remain engraved in my mind. Without further explanation or preamble, while I was staring at the sun on the horizon, I felt my lips brush against his, warming my mouth with his saliva, fresh from the temperate climate. I was stunned, speechless: she slowly moistened my lips with hers and I just enjoyed that moment. I had never been kissed by a woman before and this fascinating experience surpassed any other. She walked away from the table with a serious face.

- Manu, don't you like me? – he questioned me.

I answered myself inside: how could I not like it, if it was the most fascinating thing I had experienced up to that moment, but the unexpectedness of the event, coupled with my nerves for the first time, froze me. I could barely stammer back and knew I had to be as honest and direct as possible in that instant so as not to spoil the magical moment.

- I had never experienced anything more beautiful in my life- I was able to answer, and Aurora, hearing my nervous voice, realized what was happening and her serious face changed into a flirtatious and slightly mocking smile.

- It was your first kiss!

She put her hand on mine and I could only nod excitedly. Words no longer came out. She squeezed my hand very hard and stared at me.

- Then we'll do this.

He approached me once more and began to kiss my lips, but this time as if he wanted to devour them, as if there weren't another day to kiss me. I felt like I was short of breath, but I was fascinated with every movement of her lips and her tongue sliding over mine. After a couple of minutes she pulled away and wiped her lips with a napkin.

He looked at me penetrating my whole being and continued to give me lessons.

- So that you always remember that your first kiss was intense, not just a peak in the mouth- he turned to the girl he was serving and asked her for two glasses of wine-. Now we will toast our first kiss.

I didn't even know what to say: the physiological emotion of the kiss, the nerves of having her close, the music in the environment that seemed familiar to me, but I couldn't remember the name and the air conditioning of the place had me frozen.

- Do you like the glass of wine? - he told me while they served us.

- Of course.

At that moment I felt bowed to his will. She raised her glass and clinked mine while winking her right eye at me.

- For a moment I thought it was just a special moment for me and maybe I had rushed.

Hurried on? For me he could take out a marriage certificate at that moment and sign it. I was fascinated by everything about her.

- I know that perhaps I'm not the most handsome or intelligent man you know- I told him with nerves on the surface-, but I would like to know if you would like us to be boyfriends, or go out more, or whatever you want.

It was difficult for me to find the right words, however, for the first time I felt a tender look on her, as if following each word on my lips rhythmically and pleasantly.

"So, today will be our first day as a boyfriend," he pronounced and raised his glass again and clinked it once more with me.

- I really like that song and I think I will never forget it.

- It's Cher.

- It's true, I couldn't remember his name.

- And the song is called Jesse James. It is an analogy, where she is the bandit and intends to win the battle against her lover, just as I did here at this table, just as happened with the kiss that I gave you and that you probably would not have given me.

Chapter 7

We agreed to dedicate Friday afternoons to see each other. Sometimes in the museum or in a cafeteria on the boardwalk. In the course of time, catastrophic events occurred frequently in different parts of the world.

The glaciers were melting rapidly and the lowest parts of the planet suffered floods from which they could not fully recover. These conditions also caused the deterioration of health due to the spread of multiple diseases. It was an environment conducive to the proliferation of deadly viruses that caused two pandemics at the same time. Every so often with the outbreak of a new wave of infections, whether it was with the first or second pandemic, we had to quarantine. For us it was not a problem to spend the quarantine together. It was nothing different than what we normally did, because we spent the whole day together. We didn't need anything else from outside.

There were large earthquakes, almost daily, in some corner of the world, which left small or large cities, even countries, in ruins.

A new scale of hurricanes appeared, which was devastating. He left nothing alive in his wake.

The worsening of these natural phenomena as a whole caused serious logistical problems in all kinds of products, even basic necessities, increasing the percentage of the population that suffered from hunger.

Communication failures due to disasters developed unnatural catastrophes, such as the explosion in some fully automated industries where technology was no longer a guarantee.

Added to that, the world became a powder keg, where powerful countries took advantage of global insecurity to invade others.

There was not a single citizen in the world who did not live on alert for any event that put his life at risk. Year after year, global deaths multiplied, until they grew exponentially, which far exceeded the number of new births. The world experienced a deficit of life.

However, Gabriela and I were still together, trying to enjoy every second of life. How right she was when she told me her theory as students. It was difficult to understand that pollution does not affect the planet, but human beings. We had a totalitarian conception of the world, where the human being was the center of everything, the main being. When we were just like a microorganism inside another being. We were like the kidneys of that supreme being. We take care of filtering the blood, eliminating excess water with our actions.

At that rate, in a year, there would be no life left on the planet or the conditions for it.

Aurora and I thought about going to live far from any civilization, but we knew that there would be no place in the world where risks could not reach us.

Our country, like any third world country, was suffering from both pandemics, a militarized government, a growing wave of violence, flooding in coastal cities, and earthquakes of unprecedented magnitude. Even on September 11 of that year, a devastating earthquake was recorded in Mexico City, and despite the structural standards developed after the 1985 earthquake, the damage was much greater in the number of buildings that collapsed in the blink of an eye. blink of an eye and the number of people who lost their lives in the rubble.

We lived on the coast and there, between the problems of flooding, the criminal cartels, the poverty of the place, it was consuming everything around us. Fewer and fewer people lived in the colony, located on the outskirts of the city, near the little-visited part of the sea, perhaps that route could be a form of escape.

One day we realized that only thieves were passing by looking for food or shelter, so we had to urgently think of an alternative to be able to continue with our lives and make a family in a safe place, like the one we grew up playing in the streets with the kids from the block.

Chapter 8

A year before the debacle of the world began, Aurora and I had tried to raise awareness through various communication channels about the importance of connecting all human beings to achieve, with our energy, the goal of achieving an improvement in the world. . Using the global collective consciousness to generate positive energy that would reverse the ravages of diseases that the planet was facing.

After a few months, I became not only the person who loved her the most, but also the person who admired her the most. In a short time, it managed to be followed on the internet by more than one hundred million people from all over the world, committed to the project of producing the energy necessary to give life to the planet.

It was about millions of people who probably had small children who do not use the network, also helping the collective conscience, and probably could be multiplied by four or five from each family and acquaintances. A tenth of the world was aware of an alternative solution, perhaps unorthodox, but hopeful.

The indicators showed an improvement in the status of the planet after a few weeks of mass meditations.

The question now was, how much longer would we have to live with these actions?

No one could answer that question. There were pessimists with a couple of years of forecast; the super optimists who gave an extension of fifty years or more, or the realists who were confident that with current resources the planet could at least support ten years.

For us, ten more years was a lifetime, since she and I lived each day as if it were the last of our lives.

Many thought of taking advantage of the time given to their greatest pleasures: drinking alcohol or any exotic concoction, smoking all kinds of hallucinogens, fornicating without restraint, so that the world would end and perhaps there would not be enough time to wear out their bodies.

Despite great efforts, seeing a great improvement: people began to trust themselves and forget to contribute to awareness.

The climate gradually changed over the years, generating unexpected climatic changes. Extensions of the Earth were completely covered by water, causing serious effects on the flora and fauna, and obviously humanity was also damaged by these natural phenomena that occurred more frequently. A vicious circle was formed that deteriorated the planet, more floods, hurricanes, sinkholes, landslides, deforestation, less oxygen, pollution, earthquakes, tidal waves, diseases and more death.

The forests were consumed by fire, dramatically devastating the environment, those beautiful habitats where the most beautiful species in the world coexisted and were disappearing, generating more pollution. The beautiful landscapes were diminishing until they turned into ashes. An uninspiring scenario to poetry or life.

Those beautiful mountains bathed in snow, forming landscapes that relaxed the body to see, gradually melted, raising the sea level on each of the continents. The same happened with the wonderful glaciers, which I had the pleasure of enjoying and where I drank some whiskey with ancient ice. The forests were increasingly inhabited for their color and vegetation. The hand of man in its wake was leaving fewer and fewer places to live.

Human beings could destroy a thousand more planets, just out of ego or negligence, but they were incapable of showing solidarity and giving back to nature that incomparable beauty it possessed. The hand of man could silence the song of the birds or the most diverse and vast nuances in the feathers of the birds. I could trade the beautiful blue sky for darker shades of gray and the turquoise of the sea for a grayish brown with no marine species. He could change God's perfect creation inch by inch, just to satisfy his need for recognition. Also changing the aroma of flowers due to polluting gases from the industry and the softness of the breeze due to skin irritation due to toxic substances in the environment. And when there's nothing left, maybe it's easier to find another place to live than to renew every part of the world. Maybe when we realize it will be an unstoppable missile exploding in front of us in the form of hunger, disease and war. As we watch time go by and every day one more flower withers, one less species inhabits the planet, one more tree is consumed by the fire of some great fire caused by global warming; an uninhabitable lake that can no longer feed, an infertile land that does not germinate our hope for one more day and a difficult, dense air, impossible to breathe.

Despite everything, Aurora continued to think that the destiny of the Earth was to disappear, perhaps at a slower rate than the current one, but in the end it was just an organ within a larger being.

Chapter 9

For me, the best way to spend the few or many years that I had left to live was my daily life with her.

The routine of making love to her several times a day had me chained to her. We sometimes spent weeks without leaving home in the face of different threats.

We had become aware that each day lived was a gift from God and that at any moment everything could end, so we enjoyed ourselves to the fullest because in the end she did what I wanted and I did what she wanted, and we always wanted the same thing.

There was a warm afternoon on the balcony of our room, where we watched the sea for hours, relaxing with the cloudy sky and some raindrops splashing on us.

- We can go to another place where we can live and make a family- Aurora proposed to me.

Until then we were forbidden to talk about having children. We didn't want to leave them in a world that was dying and unsafe for them. I drank some of that low-quality, low-quality coffee, but it tasted like heaven with it.

- Beautiful, there is no other place on the planet where we can live in peace; Let's stay here and enjoy each other as long as possible- I told him trying not to be so harsh-. I don't mean Earth, let's look for a place similar to our planet to be able to make a family. This place is about to collapse.

Although it seemed crazy, the possibility of starting a family excited me too much. On multiple occasions my dreams were about a beautiful girl with blue eyes, playing to cook my food with toy kitchen utensils and with a naughty boy kicking the ball in a vast garden imitating the players of the Mexican national team. Shouting both throughout the house, filling every corner with life

- That would be perfect, what do you propose? Aurora mentioned.

- In theory, a place with similar characteristics to Earth must exist in some galaxy, I explained.

- I think the same, but it would be almost impossible, like crossing the universe to an unknown place and hoping that we can reach another kind of humanity.

- Haven't you always wanted us to have children? - I wonder. She knew she was dying to have a baby with her eyes and her smile.

- Of course, I would do anything for it. But there are no habitable places left on Earth and searching for a place in the universe is impossible.

- I know, Manuel. But if the universe is infinite, there must be another place with similar characteristics to our planet- he expressed to me with great confidence that he gave me hope to fulfill my dream of having a family one day.

- And when we find it, how will we get the resources to get to it?

- I know it sounds illogical that we can access a ship and travel to another point in the galaxy at least, and even more so that probably the ship to go further from Mars has not yet been built. But we can look for other options.

- As which?

- You're going to think I'm crazy, but I've always thought that teleportation is a possibility. Our brain must be able to do it.

She sipped her coffee trying to see my disbelieving reaction; night was beginning to fall and my hopes were somewhat dashed with her proposal, but until now she had always been right with her illogical theories.

- Well, you tell me what to do and I do it.

Although I doubted the effectiveness of her proposal, I had no choice but to embrace her.

- Let's examine. I believe that we must begin by channeling the energy that we possess in order to be able to change from one place to another.

Chapter 10

After studying day and night reclining on the balcony chair, drinking coffee to be able to read until dawn. On some occasions wine or other drinks to try to open our minds and think about all the possibilities, we coined our alternative to get to that place.

Necessity is the mother of invention, goes an old saying; in our case it made us think of all the probable alternatives, from logical ones to those that were beyond human understanding.

We had agreed that there was no way to get to the place we were looking for.

We concluded that energy was what created matter; many theories supported that assumption.

Another conclusion was that by being at levels such as those achieved by the religious to heal other people, it was possible for any human being to achieve a unique state of relaxation. We also knew that there were frequencies that evoked these states of the human being.

In this way, we were generating a model, where for each one of the senses we would be able to reach a maximum level of relaxation, that where the heart beats barely perceptible, where breathing is barely required because the universe vibrates at the same frequency as our energy, which After all, it is what forms each organ of our body.

We had to use those sounds while trying to get to that level. Breathe in a special way, slowly, to slow the heartbeat. Imagine the energy of the universe in us to attract it.

We form a kind of cabin with oxygen, as if it were a spaceship with two comfortable seats to simulate teleportation.

Every day we were adding something more so that the energy we produced was enough to get there and also key things to go to another place. What would be the essential things to travel a completely unknown place?

We carry matches and lighters to make a fire in a simple way. If on our planet fire revolutionized the world, it would probably also be essential on the other planet; obviously we think about water and various options to obtain and purify it. Without that vital element we would not survive anywhere.

He also brought other non-essential things, but they would sweeten life a little while we were away: a few bags of ground Veracruz coffee, a box of number 4 cigars, the kind we smoked when we traveled to Havana on our first-anniversary trip; a bottle of 25-year-old Scotch whiskey, which I was saving for a special occasion, and a good option would be to toast the success of our adventure, touching external soil.

He wore colored chalk to be able to make all kinds of records on any surface; also a water purification plant, thinking of supplying ourselves with many forms of the essential liquid for life; some medicines such as antibiotics and analgesics, and various sophisticated devices to measure temperature, length, height, calculate the time, ph and geolocation; maybe most of this equipment would not work where we arrived, but it was better to try and they would be very helpful in case any or most of it was used.

The religious part could not be missing; we both came from a fervently Catholic family; so we couldn't stop entrusting ourselves to a crucifix inside our makeshift nave and a rosary hanging at the head of the bed.

We had also thought about the perfect day. We understood little of these things, of the behavior of the constellations and their influence on the Earth and energy, but we tried to locate a desirable date.

The deadline was for February 23 of that year.

Chapter 11

We hermetically closed our enchanted ship, but not before crossing ourselves, entrusting ourselves to the God in whom we believed. The form of our transportation was heptagonal; for some reason she had decided that, because her favorite number was always seven. We polished each of the windows to have visibility; we had great faith that when we arrived at the place we would have a vision of everything that was happening around us.

Everything was ready. We held hands and lay on that bed where we had been together so many times. We turned on the music player to put sounds at an ideal vibration frequency so that our mind could take the trip. It was like the ignition of the ship's engines.

I insisted that a little incense could be dangerous, but she convinced me that it would help. I also agreed to your proposal to use some essential oils. Although I was skeptical, I remember a time when I had a bad cold, and she rubbed a little on my hands and my head, and I fell asleep until the next day, but I woke up one hundred percent; so nothing hurt that could help us.

We were both nervous, not because we didn't think it would work, but because we fervently believed that when we woke up from this unusual journey, we would be in an unknown place, alone and with many challenges ahead.

I tried to calm his throbbing left with a squeeze of my right hand and he relaxed; Being calm was part of the requirements to undertake this astral odyssey.

The minutes went by, while we were feeling how the environment made us go into a great relaxation.

Our bodies began to vibrate in a pleasant way, as if it were floating in the air; first slowly and then we feel a stronger and stronger ecstasy; the fingertips tickled us and caused a pleasure that completely relaxed my body; She wouldn't know at that moment what she was feeling, but in theory the same thing should happen to her.

My mind began remembering the moment I met her, and her bright eyes stared into my mind and filled my eyes with light, which, even though they were closed, each part of my body lit up and I lost track of time and space. As if levitating on my bed, I even stopped feeling the palm of his hand on mine, even knowing that it was there.

I felt like when in the movies they represent a flight at the speed of light, seeing lightning everywhere; When I started to feel an immense centrifugal force in my head, in my chest and in my calves, I knew that our dream of traveling to another place to live happily was coming true.

There came a time when I lost track of time; I could no longer find an explanation between how much a second was worth or if hours had passed; it was as if my brain was being jolted quickly, but harmoniously, with ideas and flashes passing involuntarily.

I could almost swear that moment was levitating even higher than the measurements of our ship's roof.

Little by little I was becoming aware of each part of my body; My heartbeat began to slow down until it stopped beating. It also seemed that I had stopped breathing during the entire journey and suddenly oxygen was once again entering my lungs and I was enjoying the pleasure of breathing freely.

We opened our eyes very slowly, and we automatically turned to see each other, without saying a word and we sat down to look through the misted windows and with lights coming through them that barely allowed us to perceive objects, like when you leave a dark room and look straight at the sun; the eyelids are heavy and the pupils seem to fade; little by little we were focusing, after a while remaining with the eyelids half open, until we were able to open them completely.

Chapter 12

Three hundred and sixty-five days at a speed of twenty-six thousand kilometers per hour would be a long wait for a different space. That distance and that speed marked on the electronic sensors that we carried with us.

For us it had been like the blink of an eye. We were not even sure that we had lasted all that time and at that speed; the sensors could have failed; with those parameters, our hearts could stop due to pressure variations. However, it was the only way we could rebuild our lives, just her and me. The wait would be an incomparable suffering with the pleasure of having a place to live, where we could fulfill our dreams and try a new beginning for the world.

A long wait in a space of three meters by two, so many things could happen. On the way, anxiety took over us; Doubts about our state of health, the diet that we could have to counteract the effects of not having basic elements such as the sun's rays. What would happen to the lack of mobility to which we were accustomed on Earth?

So many unknowns overwhelmed me, but there were no other alternatives but to undertake this journey of no return to an unknown place, with the daily anguish of being able to fail in the attempt. Would we be just as happy in that tiny space as we were in the green fields of the farm where we lived?

Added to this was the anguish of not knowing if the means of transportation was safe, if it would withstand the external conditions of so many places or if the fuel would be enough to avoid being lost in the immensity, gravitating and watching the seconds go by while our lives were extinguished.

The large rockets of the space expeditions had been relegated by smaller and more efficient ones in the use of resources.

We decided on the day of the launch to run along the beach, kilometers and kilometers; the most that our body will endure; I only managed to run twelve and couldn't take it anymore; she was an oak, she could run twenty five. By the time she finished, I was already waiting for her, hydrating myself, in the anteroom of the entrance to the small ship. The idea was precisely not to wait, once we finished running, to be able to enter the ship, cross ourselves and take off so that our minds would not think about it, but about the fatigue of our bodies. However, I never imagined that she had more than twice my ability and strength to run on the soft sand of the sea, where we feel the breeze on our faces; it was the most pleasant feeling we would miss when we were away.

We entered that capsule where we would spend a full year looking for a place to recreate our species. We had all kinds of small board games, video players to watch movies, video games, simulators, and despite her refusal, I decided to put a good shipment of bottles of mezcal, tequila and dark beer on board. The excuse was the upcoming celebration of his birthday, Christmas and New Years festivities, and many others that would occur to us, while we traveled towards the unknown.

Chapter 13

We almost jumped out of bed. We had to move so that our circulatory system and all our skin would work as usual. We checked all our vital signs and we were in perfect condition, even both of us showed better indicators than most, for example, our blood pressure was like that of a baby.

Up to that moment, I had known countries from almost all the continents; I walked through the glaciers of Argentina in South America. I got to know the Sequoias, those giant trees hundreds of years old located in California. I drank coffee in the jungles of Costa Rica and in Colombia, and both were delightful with their differences. I walked in the vicinity of Everest in Nepal to feel, even up close, that adrenaline of those who touch the top of the highest place on the planet. I walked a long stretch of the immense and beautiful wall of China, very cold, just wearing a long-sleeved shirt. Until that moment I had no idea that it was cold in that part of Asia.

I tried the Malay coffee, sweltering in Kuala Lumpur and its unique flavor that comes from roasting the beans with butter. I got to know the Taj Mahal, one of the most beautiful and romantic wonders of humanity, I even remember joining a dance for a couple about to get married down the street, a tradition in India; It was something like the carnival of my land in Veracruz: a whole party in the streets.

I also felt the desperation of the most chaotic traffic I had ever seen, and I think seeing more than 1.3 billion Indians was a tough record for any other country to break.

I traveled the beautiful transparent seas of Australia, without going into the water for fear of sharks. I was in Egypt seeing the pyramids and in other beautiful places in Europe, like Prague, where I tried the most exquisite beer for my palate; Perhaps it was due to the fact that for the first time my older sister, Rosi, invited me for a beer in the main square.

I obviously knew all the heterogeneous places in my country, Mexico, such as its mountains, valleys, rivers, seas, reefs, and its archaeological ruins.

However, I was greatly concerned about the climate in that place, the rainfall rate, the orography, but above all the new fauna and flora that would be our way of feeding ourselves.

We were unaware of the threats in this new environment. What would the lakes and rivers be like? Could one bathe? Would there be any dangerous or deadly animals? The temperature would be as observed or maybe the freezing point was lower and I could get into a lake. There were so many threats that passed through my head, even that of microorganisms, viruses of invisible size that had almost eradicated humanity on countless occasions, and for that reason I was afraid to even breathe out there. Or the toxic gases that this new environment could contain could slowly damage my body, as the industries did, deteriorating the health of millions of people who died of cancer. The fear was great, but we had already taken the first step: travel hundreds of thousands of kilometers outside the universe to find a new home.

We didn't know how our tired body would respond to being without movement, or without having the vitamins and minerals that sunlight produces through the atmosphere. It had been a long wait, the longest of our lives, but nevertheless every minute with her was a reason to try everything. That's why I didn't think twice and having passed the fears of the long trip, now those of the new world stalked me. I had to take care of her, it was almost like starting civilization again, like going back to the cave era, where I had to protect her from the outside, in the same way as the first human beings, without knowing what the threats of nature were. From the window of the capsule where we traveled, a place very similar to Earth in color was seen; the atmosphere was sunny, a sign that it was daytime; We did not know how long day and night lasted in that place. At first you could see the green ground, like when you fly over where there are many trees, but as we got closer they had a different structure. The trees had a pyramidal shape; the root was like a triangle that narrowed with height. That difference caused me tension, but I was sure that we would both be able to overcome any obstacle.

Chapter 14

I remembered that historic moment when Armstrong became the first man to set foot on the moon. I didn't want to put my name in future history books, I just wanted to live happily with her. That is why I thought that she should be the one to take the first step on the New Earth, as we had chosen to call this new place where we could repopulate humanity. However, I was stressed that that first step was in a muddy place and I could have an accident; At first glance it looked like safe ground, but we didn't have 100 percent accuracy, since we had never been in that place.

The color of the ground was greenish; just as that of Mars was reddish, that of this planet Earth had a greenish color, blending a little with turquoise. When she took that step I felt terrified, even more so when she made a moan of emotion, which I confused with one of concern; each time I advanced entrenched on a different colored but firm ground, it calmed me down; I did not imagine the kind of fruits that could emanate from that land.

We began to build a small house around the capsule, with the few materials we had, adding a bit of what we got to know as the days went by. In fact, the sand on the ground was thick and compacted very strongly. It was the essential element to be able to have shelter. We did not know how intense the winds could be. So far there was hardly a blizzard blowing. It was very nice weather. We began to write down everything to discover the seasonality. At the moment we arrived we did not know if it was the coldest or hottest season. The climate was, according to my perception, like on Earth. It was about seventeen degrees Celsius. I wish we were in the spring or autumn season, because if it was summer in its warmest phase, we would probably have a winter that was too cold and for which we did not have the necessary clothing. At night, it would feel like four degrees of temperature, and we slept dressed, in thick clothes, so as not to feel cold.

In the first rain that we had to live, we observed every slight detail; We knew that our subsistence depended on the historical information of everything that happened at every moment; We even collected some rainwater to analyze its characteristics in the devices that we managed to include in the ship to see if it was possible to drink it in that state. In the first days we discovered two things that made us a little happy: first, that rainwater had enviable characteristics; it was drinkable and, apart from that, it had all the qualities of salts and minerals that were perfect for the body, even better than water in its best state on Earth. The second pleasant piece of news was that, during the rain, the ground quickly absorbed the water, and the ground was not muddy and could be walked on without problems.

Every day we walked a diameter of one kilometer in relation to the capsule so as not to stray too far and to discover the new characteristics of this planet of which we were unaware of everything; all we knew was that its conditions were the closest thing to Earth's atmosphere. When we reached three kilometers we would begin to walk deeper, one day in each direction of the cardinal points

The first kilometer that we traveled was a beautiful, colorful valley and everything was similar in terms of weather and soil conditions. We were drawing a map from each kilometer that we were increasing.

Chapter 15

We began to carry out experiments with what seemed like seeds that we obtained from the fruits that we were discovering to plant them and see if they flourished like on Earth, thinking in the future of harvesting our own food. We discovered flowers of an impressive color and we observed how they changed their hue. It was quite a sight to behold. There were colors that we did not know existed and were not made from some combination of the primary colors. Until then we had not found animal species, only birds, and we feared the appearance of some dangerous animal.

Fortunately, we had a life to know our new home and that made the days interesting, besides living with her was always a pleasure.

Nights at that time of year only lasted six hours, which is why we had the routine of making love at sunset, with the sunset as a showcase, and then resting to get up the next day and continue our expedition.

Every day we were better; We did not know everything about the place: if there was a greater or lesser gravity than on Earth, or an unbearable atmospheric pressure. I don't know if the environment or the feeding behavior in our bodies would affect us, but I was sure I could make love to her up to four times during the night. In reality, he lived in ecstasy and in paradise.

We worked very hard during the day, from sunrise to sunset, because we knew that soon we would start to be more people and that entailed greater care and responsibility. On it depended the resurgence of our race. Regardless of this crucial mission, our greatest desire was to form a beautiful family and live happily by their side.

After traveling three kilometers in diameter, we decided, from the fourth, to walk towards each of the cardinal points to advance faster.

Chapter 16

On the seventh day I decided to walk along a path formed by rocks and trees from the east side to our position. It did not seem like a path made on purpose, but the symmetry in which various elements were combined to draw a constant line for a section until it was lost when turning around was very marked. I had a backpack with me with the essentials for the journey and a sensor to measure each section. When I turned around where the view of the road was lost, the route continued in the same symmetrical way. I walked for several minutes, when the indicator marked almost three kilometers, more lighting seemed to be seen in the background, indicating a wider place where the path ended or perhaps it became larger. I couldn't see exactly what was at the end, it just looked brighter in shades of green. As I got closer, a beautiful lake began to appear, but a very light green color, perhaps it had adopted the color of the surrounding flora, which was a strong green combined with various gradients. The infinity of flowers everywhere, the large and appetizing fruits, the extended branches for several meters. Even the rocks of various sizes adorning the surrounding area were grayish-green. Also the birds of different species that flew over the sky, showed that tone and some animals similar to reptiles that wandered in the distance also had that coloration.

Like a surreal painting, infinite, and although being monochromatic might seem boring, there were millions of shades, but always with a characteristic green. You felt absolute relaxation, especially when the calm, crystalline water ran, whose sound hypnotized. I extracted some coffee from my thermos from my backpack and decided that it was the ideal place to drink some, while enjoying a cool breeze and the delicious humidity that refreshed my entire body, even the sky was also seen with a touch of green.

At the bottom of the lake with an almost rectangular shape, another path was observed; it looked woody green; I would no longer have time to go through it, although my curiosity was killing me to know if this green carnival had several more kilometers; I decided to walk it calmly another day, already knowing the first path traveled.

I was tempted to eat that appetizing-looking, almost fluorescent, bright-colored apple, but decided not to risk it; Instead I put it in my light luggage and walked back, step by step, amazed that such a place existed. I also had not realized that the color of the sand also had a touch of that tone, it even changed automatically when leaving the path of trees and rocks. At that time, as a man of science that I always tried to be, the theory that it was an effect caused by sunlight began to arise, because just as we left the last tree on the path behind, that coloration began to intensify on the sand. I did not want to go back. That place attracted me, but nevertheless, I had to return. I imagined that if he was perfect alone, next to her he would be immaculate, so I ran back to tell him and everything, and on the way I imagined myself with her.

The aroma of the flowers disappeared instantly upon crossing that threshold and one of humidity from the rocks and the wood of the trees combined appeared.

The last few meters I ran towards her, excited, yelling at her how beautiful that place was that she had to accompany me. She couldn't even sleep thinking about what he told her about that magical place. For this reason, as soon as the first rays of the sun began to appear, we got out of bed and walked towards that natural path.

And so we did the next day, we camped there. Her drawing at times the green nature around, in an oil that she brought with her and some colored crayons. While I drank mezcal lying on the sand with that delicious breeze. He lied saying that he was recording information about the place in a notebook, but he was writing a poem for her. It was the ideal moment to dedicate some beautiful words to them. The scent of flowers that day was even deeper, but light. It was like feeling the scent of roses, very light in the air. There were even flowers similar in shape, but without petals and a very soft green color.

With an hour to go before dark, by our reckoning, I snatched the Colors from her hands and started kissing her. We couldn't miss out on that paradise to make love to her, aside from the fact that it was time to start thinking not only about having sex or making love, both of which were a delight to be with her. Now we also had to start doing it religiously to have the family that I had always dreamed of with her, ever since I fell in love with her gaze.

Chapter 17

I had a beautiful lucid dream. I felt a peace that I had never experienced. I dreamed of a forest of leafy trees, surrounded by hundreds of multi-colored plants, from where a woman with perfect features and a dark complexion appeared.

I felt great peace being close to her and she began to talk to me about I don't know why because I couldn't hear her, although in my dream I did understand what she was saying because she also moved her lips as if responding to her.

He hugged me and placed in my hands a fruit of an appetizing color, like that of a cherry with a greenish touch, but larger in size and of such shine that it seemed that an elixir of exquisite juice would flow from one bite.

I immediately devoured it, not leaving a drop of juice inside. I felt how it was cooling from the tip of my tongue to every part inside me. A delicious sensation. When that woman saw me happy, she smiled with a cute image, but with a malicious touch, and turned around to disappear.

Inside I began to feel that something was beginning to grow in an immediate and inexplicable way, as if I had devoured a gas bomb and was about to explode. A few minutes later blood was coming out of my mouth and I was slowly fainting. With each step I doubled over until I fell face down expelling more and more things inside me, until I was breathless.

There are so many theories of dreams, from those that say that they have no meaning. Some are only images related to day-to-day life, even those that claim that they can be revelations or predictions of the dreamer's life.

With that image drilling my senses, I woke up that fresh morning, even colder than the previous days. I couldn't anticipate a change of season, maybe it was just a cold front like the ones that used to be on Earth. We decided that day to record the weather and various other features from our ship so as not to expose ourselves to any radical change in weather.

I took the opportunity to open one of the mezcal bottles and put on some music, while I watched her record every little detail of that day. Immersed, doing what she liked best, it was a delight to watch her. I liked her face more every day and also her fine body. Each sip of mezcal was an aphrodisiac for that night.

As much as I tried to get his attention, he didn't flinch, despite the loud sound of the music or my movement as I took each sip from my glass.

His favorite song could not fail: so I dived into the suitcase where we keep the compact discs to find his musical weakness. I loved the classical and hated the popular sounds, except that song by Jenny Rivera. I almost swore that in the choir he would forcefully turn to see me and sing those verses to me.

"And enough of your unconsciousness in that absurd way of seeing daily how you throw away my heart, what I give you. And enough yaaaaa..."

I didn't get those dedicated verses, but I did get his attention with a similar retort.

- Aren't you going to help me at all, lazy? - told me. And we both laugh at his peculiar way of referring to me. Those holes that were made in his cheeks shone with the little sun of the day. I brought the mezcal up to my nose and inhaled the aroma it gave off, while without looking at her I said:

- That's why I have my slaves to work for me.

Immediately, I turned around to turn my back and see how at that moment the sun and the moon could be seen at the same time. I was sure that would provoke a pleasant irritation in her at my defiant response, and it did.

He pounced on me, grabbing me by the waist; He let his body fall and with the force of his weight he turned me around and threw me onto the bed. He looked at me with red eyes and it wasn't courage. I could see through them their wishes to kiss me.

"In this moment, we will see who is the slave of whom," she released me. And he began to bite my lips in a wild way, first stripping my torso and then unbuttoning my pants.

- And why am I the only one without clothes? - I managed to whisper, with my breath stolen by his oppressive kisses.

- Because you are my slave, bitch.

She climbed on top of me and immediately took off her blouse, and lifted her skirt up to where I was able to get into it a little forced by the discomfort of the fabric of her underwear. Seeing her on top of me, with her immense legs at my sides and her closed-eyed face moving with gestures of pleasure, was a perfect image. It was difficult to contain the desire to finish quickly, but I had to do it to continue enjoying that moment and that scene with her pursed lips.

She fell exhausted next to me, leaning on my shoulder, her breath agitated. I felt more than tired, ecstatic, happy to have made her explode with pleasure.

- Now yes, tell me who is the slave of whom?

Why did I say that? She got up as if driven by a spring and pounced on me again, kissing me...

- At this time we will see ...

Chapter 18

It was an immense happiness to live in that place with her. After seven months of being in that place, we had begun to notice a constant pattern in the change in ambient temperature that allowed us to conclude that we were in the coldest season of the year.

She began to eat less than other days, and to worry me; I was also nervous about the fact that he had been returning everything he ate for several days. It scared me to think that some virus from that place was harming her. She noticed my extreme concern every time we ate, precisely at the time when the sun pointed to the natural path that led to the place where everything was green.

Every time he tried to reach a plate, with some fruit or vegetable, he immediately brought it closer. He would ask Aurora if she wanted to drink some water and he would serve it to her immediately.

In such a short time, with the investigations we had done, we knew almost everything about the operation of the place. We had also noticed an improvement in our state of health. Since our arrival, the quality of the air was so pure that taking a breath was a delight like drinking the water from that place or resting in the green area. The food, perhaps due to the low contamination, was pure medicine for our body, and the changes in temperature, which for years caused us extreme allergies, to the point of irritating our eyes and skin, had ended.

That is why his notable change in health caused me such surprise. He remembered the great epidemics in the previous world, where a microorganism killed millions of people because they did not know how to attack it.

That idea wouldn't let me sleep and she noticed it, but that day I watched her with a pale face. Everything he ate he gave back. So he began to choose what to eat without affecting him and to drink a lot of water.

Despite his contorted face, every time he drank water he turned to look at me and gave me a sarcastic smile, and winked at me. I was holding my hair thinking what would go through his mind. In order not to stress myself so much, I decided to integrate some tequila with lemon and salt into my meal to relax, while I figured out how I could help her. I tried not to let go of my head the idea that one day I could be left alone.

And suddenly he was staring at me, and now the one who turned pale was me.

- What's up, Aurora? You feel good? - I asked, while my heart began to beat rapidly.

- Better than ever.

- We must see how to relieve you. You can't go on with that disease we don't know about. It can damage any organ.

- Don't worry about me, I'll be fine. I know when I will recover.

- When? What organ did you damage? - I told him trying to be patient and took another sip of tequila. She drank the entire glass of water on the table. That again generated a deluge of adrenaline in my body.

- Well, get ready to take care of this disease that has damaged my heart. It will only be the next nine months.

Without saying a word I took the bottle of tequila. I completely filled my glass to the brim and drank it all in one gulp. Only in a cry of joy that he could swear had been heard all over the planet, there he was sitting paralyzed with his whole body vibrating with emotion.

She didn't know whether to run and hug her because she would squeeze her so hard that she didn't even want the wind to bother her.

I approached her slowly and gently placed my head on hers.

- Thank you; love you.

- You love me? Or do you love us? - he said laughing.

- I love you and our future baby infinitely.

- Or our babies. Can be

- That would be perfect; so one stays with you and the other I take with me to accompany me around the planet.

I was beginning to fantasize about the family I always dreamed of, the life I always wanted.

- We did not bring music for babies; you will have to sing

She knew that she had planned this trip perfectly.

- Did we bring?

I got up from the table and went right to the place and to the suitcase where I had kept those records with music for babies. It was the first thing that had started; without dreams there is no life, and my dream was always that.

Chapter 19

From that day on, I would get up an hour earlier and return an hour later. I didn't like leaving her alone for so long, but now I had to think of not only two, but at least three people, and have the necessary provisions because, although we already have many characteristics of the place, we still didn't know if there would be a colder season where we would have what to winter

My concern is that they were running out of spare parts to determine edible foods in a way that's not as accurate, but at least safer than chance. However, there would come a time when we would always have to opt for the same breaths or try to risk trying others without evaluating them. Navigation systems were not working on site and for this reason we had no idea of the size of the New Earth. At a certain point we decided not to explore anymore and settle in that place looking to provide enough plowing for that land. Even if the new Earth was only 10 percent the size of the old one, we would never be able to cover even a tiny piece of it by walking. Otherwise it was bigger, the task seemed impossible.

We arrived at May 29 of our calendar that we had, of which we still did not know if this measurement system was also applicable here, since we did not know if the star that illuminated us rotated in translation or the speed at which the new Earth carried out the rotation about its own axis. We both decided that it would be my last day exploring and from then on we would both dedicate ourselves to taking care of the fruit of our love for the remaining five months.

That day I tried to go through the most leafy place that we had traveled in search of more options to feed ourselves.

I had so many different fruits and vegetables in my suitcase, as a family man I had to try to feed each member as much as possible.

My back ached, but fortunately, after noon, the maximum temperature was two degrees. The cold allowed me to walk even more since I did not have the usual heat of the previous Earth and also served to warm me up to counteract the icy climate.

He was only wearing a thick long-sleeved shirt with thermal clothing under the shirt and pants.

I felt sweaty inside, but on the outside an intense cold on my cheeks. I was eating some fruits on the way and that gave me energy apart from enjoying the exquisite flavors of the place.

From the moment I looked between the branches of that tree I fell in love with its fruit. It was of a color that I couldn't describe among those known to us humans. His skin shone in the sun and the raindrops still present from the light rain hours before made him want more.

It was slightly larger than the average size of a watermelon, albeit square in shape and an exotic color. It was similar in texture to a watermelon and slightly larger in size, albeit rectangular in shape instead of circular.

It no longer fit in my suitcase so I had to carry it four kilometers back to the ship.

I did not feel the weight of that voluptuous fruit along the way, nor the cold of the wind increasing with each step, until a little new, thin snow began to fall, but I hurried to share with her this perfect-looking fruit.

I remembered Christmas in our previous world and a few tears escaped my cheeks when I remembered my parents and grandparents sitting at the table with Christmas music, and the taste of fritters.

When I saw the ship almost two hundred meters away, a little covered in white crystals by snow, I hastened even more; I had drawn strength from deep within me and the only thing I wanted was to be rested with her by my side, a good coffee and savoring that delicacy that I was carrying.

She hugged me emotionally when she arrived, much more than before, squeezing me tight and with tears in her eyes.

- It must be Christmas- he whispered in my ear.

I smiled too, with a tear in my eyes and we stayed for minutes embracing.

Chapter 20

At night the cold was greater. We decided to make a kind of fireplace to feel a little warm. We both had a thick blanket over our shoulders that hung all over our bodies.

That cold made us remember how important it was to make a family. Despite being completely alone, we could value what we had and affirm that we had reached a point where we both became completely happy. After having quickly analyzed that fruit, since we were dying to eat it, we broke it up and put it on the table to share it.

I uncovered a bottle of wine and poured two glasses, although only one would be drunk. She had to take care of herself for the next few months for our descendant. Night had fallen and there we were reclining on an improvised chair made in the new Earth, with a very resistant wood and with the characteristic of being also soft. Something hard to find on ancient Earth.

We had also built a small table to put it in front of the armchair, where every afternoon we drank wine or coffee, while we watched the sunset of the new Sun, we were still not sure if it was the same sun of the Earth or it was another star with the characteristics very similar. The truth is that when it set it looked like a fireworks display every day.

I made Aurora a cup of hot chocolate. There were few servings left and above all without expiration and she had kept them only to pamper her as long as possible, because her fascination was drinking it every afternoon. That aroma "killed" me, but I had to abstain so that it would last longer. I gave her the honor of trying that fruit that I had discovered that afternoon and she took it in her hands and began to devour it. Apparently he had liked her too much.

- Do you want more? - I asked him while I brought another large piece to his mouth. Watch out and bite my fingers, love.

- Do not be a clown!

He was smiling at me with his thick lips and I felt like the fullest man in the world, the old one and the new one.

She tried to kiss me with her lips dripping from the juice of that delicious food and she pounced on me. I tried to touch her belly, afraid of hurting our baby, and when she put her hands on my cheeks the pieces of fruit accidentally fell to the floor of the ship.

"I'm sorry" she told me and began to cry, probably due to the effect of the hormones caused by the pregnancy. I hugged her and kissed her delicately.

- It doesn't matter, love, it doesn't matter. I'm fine, drinking wine. I brought that fruit especially for you.

- Forgive me. Tomorrow we will go out and I will accompany you to look for another one so that you can enjoy it too.

She felt too sorry for something that didn't matter to me. Really the taste of the wine had taken away my appetite and having his gaze in front of me, with the sunset, was enough to be satisfied.

- No, we won't go out anymore. Here we will make our home. That's where we had stayed. Someday we will eat that fruit again, but with our children.

- I feel bad for wasting your work today.

It wasn't my job today. I brought more things, don't worry. Please believe me, it doesn't matter to me. Only now you have already tried something more in life than me. Now we only have to think about our future baby; so let's get on with the evening; I will break other fruits that I brought and I will make some coffee for myself.

Chapter 21

I woke up with a terrible headache. I was trying to get used to the idea that it was the hangover from the bottle of wine we drank the day before, although it felt different and more intense. I got out of bed quietly so as not to wake Aurora. I made some coffee in one pot and in another some chocolate.

Everything was clouded by the snow that fell and covered the branches of the trees and the windows of our ship. It was a bit like Christmas morning in the old world, when we woke up with winter on our shoulders and with cold hands, we drank coffee and chocolates, while we opened the presents listening to the classic Christmas songs.

I finished preparing breakfast and Aurora was still wrapped in sheets from the cold. It was weird that I hadn't woken up to the delicious smell of my baked muffins or freshly made frothy chocolate.

I called her a couple of times and she didn't answer me, so I sat on the sofa looking out the window at the snow, while I drank my coffee. I didn't want to wake her. In his state he had to keep as much rest as possible.

With the intense cold and despite the caffeine, I fell exhausted in the chair with two blankets on top and with the cup in hand.

I don't know how many hours passed, but it was already late afternoon when I opened my eyes. My head ached and I felt slightly feverish.

Aurora was still lying on the bed. She had slept too much, so I went over to touch her forehead to see if she wasn't irritated like me.

It was like an unexpected blow. Her cheeks were not irritated, but cold; maybe she was too cold, I took another two blankets and put them on her, while I got into bed with her and my feet touched hers, which were almost frozen.

- Aurora, Aurora, Aurora, are you okay?

I did not receive an answer. I shook her head to try to wake her up. I felt his pulse and it was very slow. His blue eyes opened for a fraction of a second, he stared at me and tried to smile, but he didn't finish it and closed them again. I felt her pulse again and checked her breathing. I ran like crazy to put the oxygen we had saved and try to revive her. I didn't understand what was happening, I just knew that I couldn't lose her, I couldn't lose my family after going through the entire universe for her.

I spent the entire afternoon and night trying to revive her, giving her breathless mouth-to-mouth dozens of times, pressing her chest, but all to no avail. The sun began to rise and she was still motionless on the bed. The only thing I had eaten that day was that beautiful fruit that I found on my last day exploring the place.

I spent two days hugging her body, without eating or drinking anything, I just wanted to go with her to the place where she was. I had no strength at all. Hours before he was the happiest man in the world, and now the most unfortunate.

His body was getting colder. I was going to stay there until I stopped breathing next to him.

I tried to decipher the expression of his last look before he fainted. It was different from other occasions, although it did not denote pain or sadness, on the contrary, I saw something else, but I could not decipher it.

I took from her beautiful neck the pendant that I gave her on her birthday, when I told her to always wear it to remember me, even though I was no longer present. She made a sad face and told me with her unique voice:

- If something happens to me one day, I would like to see you happy and continue with your life. That would make me immensely happy wherever I was.

I got out of bed, packed a travel suitcase with the most essentials and decided to be a nomad. To walk eternally, traveling the planet, alone, with Aurora in my thoughts.

END

If you liked the novel, I would appreciate it if you gave me a review and consult the author's other works here: http://amazon.com/author/jrcaamano